PRINCESS OF PETALS

GRIMM ACADEMY #15

LAURA GREENWOOD

CONTENTS

BLURB

Astrid has known for years about her prophecy, and when her parents send her to the prestigious Grimm Academy, she hopes she might finally be able to put it behind her.

Despite her parents' insistence that she comes away with a noble suitor, she can't help but find herself drawn to Conan, a scholarship student with a prophecy of his own he's trying to avoid.

When the Bellpoint Castle competition to find an heir comes along, she finally feels as if she might have found a solution to her problems. If she wins, she'll be a princess, and able to choose her own suitor. If she loses, then she could fall prey to her prophecy and lose it all.

Princess Of Petals is a fantasy academy romance inspired by the Beauty and the Beast fairy tale. It is part of the Grimm Academy series. It includes a sweet m/f romance.

PROLOGUE

I make my way into the kitchen and set down the basket of apples I've collected from the market.

"Astrid, will you sit for a moment?" Mother asks.

I turn, surprised to find both of my parents at the table, seeming to be waiting for me.

I leave the basket and take a seat opposite them. "Is everything all right?" I ask, looking between them and trying to figure out what's happening.

"It's about your prophecy."

I freeze, a sense of dread flooding through me. My prophecy has been hanging over my head since the moment I learned it.

"Nobody has given me a rose," I assure them both.

"We know," Mother responds.

"You've been offered a place at Grimm Academy," Father says.

I stare at him, not quite believing what he's saying. Everyone knows about Grimm Academy. To say it's prestigious would be an understatement.

"Are you certain?" I ask, unable to come to terms with the idea that somewhere like Grimm would be interested in someone like me. My parents are very successful merchants, but nothing compares to the lineage of being born into nobility. Or better yet, royalty.

"We're certain," Mother says.

"But why? Surely there are better potential students in the area."

"That isn't a question we thought wise to ask the messenger," Mother says.

"Ah, yes." I glance down at my lap, not wanting to draw attention to how bad it is to have asked the question in the first place.

"It is going to cost us a lot of money to send you there," Mother continues. "We expect you to make the most of it."

"Do you have any classes you particularly wish for me to take?"

Mother lets out a small squeak of annoyance. "Not with your classes, Astrid."

"What your mother is trying to say is that we would appreciate it if you turned your attention to trying to make a betrothal arrangement with a young noble, or the heir to a title."

"You want me to go to one of the best academies in the kingdom and focus on getting married instead of learning everything I can?" A small part of me is in complete disbelief about what they're suggesting. I would have thought they'd prefer it if I could learn from the best teachers around so that I can help their shops thrive even more once I return.

"It is the next step for our family, Astrid. You know how much of an advantage it will be for us to say that our daughter is married to a noble."

"I don't want to marry because it's good for business," I protest.

Mother slams her hand against the table. "You will do what we tell you, Astrid. You are being given an opportunity that we would have killed for when we were your age. Your sister too."

My stomach sinks as I think about how Kirsten is going to be taking this. She's never liked it when I get things she doesn't, I can't imagine she is going to be particularly pleased about this.

"What if I refuse to go?"

"Astrid," Mother scolds. "You are going. And we will be visiting to make sure you hold up your end of the deal."

"Doesn't a deal have two sides to it?" I mutter.

"What did you say?" Mother demands.

"I was saying that I would," I lie, not seeing any point in trying to reason with them when they're clearly not wishing to be reasoned with. "I'll make the most of what Grimm Academy has to offer."

That part isn't an untruth. I do intend to do that, even if it isn't in the way they quite want me to. But I'm fully aware of the difference an education like the one I could get at the academy will make to my life.

"Very good. You'll leave in three days."

"Three days?" I echo. "That isn't very long."

"Is there anything that would need your attention for longer than that?" Mother asks.

I shake my head. "I'm just surprised by how little time they've given us to prepare."

"Well, this is the situation, accept it for what it is and make sure you're ready. You can pick out some fabrics for dresses."

"Thank you." No doubt they'll wish for me to at least look the part while I'm trying to capture the attention of a noble they deem good enough.

I hope they quickly grow bored of their plan to visit, that way I'll be left to my own devices as much as possible. Perhaps then I'll have an enjoyable time at the academy.

"May I be excused?" I ask. "I have much to pack if I'm to leave so soon." Especially if I need new dresses too.

Mother nods.

I rise to my feet. "Thank you for this wonderful opportunity." Despite their stipulations, I actually mean it. This could make a huge difference to my life, and I'm happy that I get an opportunity to go somewhere like Grimm at all.

I leave the room and head out into the shop so I can pick the fabrics for the dresses I'll need. A small part of me doesn't want to take advantage of Mother's offer, but I know I'm going to need the wardrobe change if I'm going to fit in with the royalty I'll be spending time with.

The fabric store is blissfully empty, meaning I can spend my time examining each of the fabrics in turn. This is my favourite part of my parents' business, not that they have any idea. That would involve them actually paying more attention to me than they currently do.

I pull out several bolts of fabric, mostly those that I know will create dresses that don't wear quickly, but will look good quality. They aren't as flashy as those my sister or mother would choose, but they suit me just fine.

Someone clears their throat behind me, and I turn to find Kirsten leaning against the door frame.

"Is everything all right, sister?" I ask, setting another bolt of fabric on the workstation.

"Mother says you're leaving."

"Yes."

"Hmm." There's a note of something undefined in her voice. I can't put a name to it, but I do know that I don't like it.

Then again, that is just a summary of the way my older sister feels about me.

"I'm leaving in three days."

"Which means we're going to be left making sure all of your orders are fulfilled." She crosses her arms.

I grimace. "The time frame is not my choice." Neither is leaving home, though I can't say I'm particularly upset about that.

"It is still inconsiderate of you."

I turn away from her and roll my eyes. It's not entirely fair for me to be angry at her when I know my parents have chosen to keep my prophecy from her. I think they believe it will protect her from having to worry about it, but I don't think it has done either of us any favours and has just created a distance between us.

If I'm honest with myself, it'll be nice to get away from her, though I'm sure it will make her insufferable for the next few days.

Though I suppose there's no getting around that, even if I want to.

CHAPTER 1

The castle is bustling with activity as the various students either make their way to class, or to the welcome meeting that's being put on. There are no terms here to accommodate the holidays of all the various kingdoms, but according to my welcome information, there is a group of us all starting today.

It makes me feel less alone in finding my way around. The grounds are far vaster than I expected them to be, and I'm still not sure about some of the social expectations that come with being at the academy. Supposedly, titles don't mean anything here, but I'm not naive enough to think that just because they *say* that's the case, that it actually is.

A servant approaches. "Mistress Astrid?" she checks.

"Yes."

"Follow me, please." She gestures for me to follow her through a large set of double doors and into what appears to be a ballroom, though thankfully, it doesn't seem to be being used in that way today. While I know the theory of dancing, and enjoy it, I can't imagine I'm going to be as good as I need to be.

We approach a young woman about my age, and the servant clears her throat. "Your Highness," the servant says, dipping into a curtsy and confirming my suspicion about titles in one breath.

The woman turns to us and smiles warmly. "How can I help, Delia?" she asks the servant, a slight accent to her voice that I can't place. Which is unusual. I'm used to dealing with people from all over the various kingdoms in my parents' shops, I recognise most of them by this point.

"This is Mistress Astrid, a new student here," she says. "The headmistress informed me that I should introduce the two of you."

"Thank you, Delia, I'll take it from here."

The servant dips into a curtsy and hurries away.

"Hello," the other woman says to me. "I'm Cordelia."

"Astrid." I pause for a moment, considering whether I should ask about her title. I don't want to insult her by asking, but I also don't want to insult her by getting it wrong, which puts me in a bit of a difficult situation, and I'm not sure what to do about it.

"You want to ask me if you need to start calling me *Your Highness*, right?" Cordelia guesses.

"How did you know?"

"I had the same confusion when I got here," she admits. "The servants use titles, but most of the students and teachers don't. It's confusing when you first get here, but you get used to it."

"So you have one?"

"A title? Technically, yes. In reality, I'm a homeless princess who will never inherit, I'm not sure how useful that is."

"I'm a merchant's second daughter if that helps?"

She chuckles. "Perhaps it does. Anyway, I'm assigned to show you and another new student around."

"You're not new?"

She shakes her head. "I came here about half a year ago when my older sister averted her prophecy," she says. "It's a long story. I'll tell it to you some time."

It takes a few more minutes for the other student to arrive, accompanied by the same servant who showed me into the room.

"Hi." She gives us a nervous wave. "I'm Elisa."

"I'm Cordelia, this is Astrid," our guide introduces herself. "Shall we get to the tour?"

"Is the headmistress not going to talk to us?" I ask.

Cordelia shakes her head and gestures for us to follow her. "Most of the time, she leaves the students to their own devices. If she needs to speak with you, then you'll get a summons to her office."

"What kind of things make that happen?" Elisa asks.

"Mostly prophecy stuff. You'll find that most of the staff only deal with their own classes, and they're not very strict on most of the rules, which makes it nice and easy to live our lives."

"That's good to know," I say. "Not that I plan on breaking any of the rules."

Cordelia lets out a light laugh. "I don't think many students here plan on breaking the rules, but I suspect many of them do when it comes to dealing with their prophecies. Which is probably why they're so lax."

"Do many of the students here have them?" I ask, thinking of the reputation the academy has for dealing with students in the same position as I'm in.

"Allegedly, but no one really talks about it," Cordelia says. "And the staff aren't allowed to interfere directly with the prophecies either. Though according to some of the older students, they'll often plan lessons around a situation if they know someone is in one."

I frown. "But how do they know?"

"There's a book of prophecies in the head-mistress' office according to my sister."

"And let's guess, we're not allowed to look in it?" Elisa says.

"No."

"They're making solving prophecies particularly difficult," she mutters.

Cordelia's amusement flits right over her face, making me feel very at ease around the princess, even if she's much higher up the social status than I am.

I know it's early to think that I might have a connection with someone here, but it's certainly starting to feel that way.

Then again, maybe this is why they've asked Cordelia to be the one to show people around, she might just be genuinely nice.

"Have you found your chambers yet?" Cordelia asks.

I nod. "I'm on the second floor of the east tower."

"Ah, me too," Elisa says.

"Same. They must have taken that into account when they decided to ask me to be the one to show you around," Cordelia says. "It'll certainly make things easier for us. I can show you the best way down to the dining hall for breakfast tomorrow, and we can focus on the rest of the grounds today."

"Is there much to see?" Elisa asks.

Cordelia leads us out of the castle and into the grounds. "It depends what you're interested in. There's a lake."

Elisa freezes. "Are there swans on it?"

"I don't think so," Cordelia responds. "Or at least, there aren't any that I've ever seen. Why?"

"I don't like them very much," Elisa says.

For a moment, I wonder whether it's something to do with a prophecy. She hasn't said that she has one, but she did bring them up before, and the chances are high that any particular student has one.

"I'll ask around just to be sure," Cordelia promises. "Anyway, the Huntsmen practice in the woods, and I think they have a camp in there too, but they're not the only ones who are allowed in it. So if you like midnight strolls that take you through a wooded area, that's the place to go."

"Is that safe?" I ask. "Mother always told me not to go walking in the woods alone."

"It's as safe as a wood is going to be," she points out. "The Huntsmen are there, which offers a good level of protection, and then there are the Grimm Academy guards. They'll follow you into the village if you go there too to make sure you're kept safe."

"We're allowed to just go around like that?"

"Mmhmm. Grimm believes that the older students like us need to be given the freedom to live our own lives. I think it's different for the younger students, but I didn't study here when I was that age, so it's impossible to know for sure."

She leads us around the academy, showing us both the grounds, and the castle itself. I'm used to people coming and going from the shop all the time, but this is different. There are people every-where I look, and they're all going about their daily lives without a care in the world.

They probably don't even realise there are new students arriving.

It doesn't take long for my new arrival nerves to start fading and for the conversation with the two others to start flowing. Perhaps it is just circum-stance that makes me feel as if they're easy to get along with, but I don't think so. Sometimes, it's possible to just tell that people are a good fit, and I get that from Elisa and Cordelia. Certainly more than I've ever gotten from anyone back home, in-cluding my sister.

If this is what my life at Grimm Academy is going to be like, then it's going to be everything I hoped and more.

CHAPTER 2

I step into the classroom, trying to ignore how nervous I am about being here and wishing that either Cordelia or Elisa could be with me. It may only have been a few weeks since my arrival at the academy, but it's clear to me that the two of them are going to be my lifelong friends.

Unfortunately, that doesn't help me when I have to go to my *Introduction to Court Etiquette* class that's required for all students who aren't nobles or royalty, and considering it turns out that Elisa is also a princess, neither of them actually need it.

I take a seat in the middle of the rows of chairs, trying not to feel self-conscious about being here. Everyone is in the same position of not having any clue what they're doing amongst the higher-ranked students, so it's not like I'm going to make too big a fool of myself.

The class fills up with about fifteen other students, which is more reassuring than I want to admit to it being.

"Hey," someone says as they sit down beside me.

"Hi." My nerves don't go anywhere, especially when the owner of the voice is a handsome young man about my age, with a smile that can break hearts.

"I'm Conan."

"Astrid."

"Have you been at the academy long?" he asks, his tone and demeanour putting me a little more at ease.

"A few weeks. What about you?"

"Around the same. I'm here on a scholarship," he admits somewhat sheepishly.

"I have no idea how that works," I admit. "I'm just a merchant's daughter."

"A successful one, by the look of your dress," he responds. "Wait, sorry, that didn't sound good. That's not what I meant."

"It's all right, I appreciate someone being able to recognise fabrics," I say, smoothing out the fabric and trying not to feel self-conscious about how rich it looks. "It's my favourite part of working in my parents' shops. I suppose it means that my dresses look a little bit fancier than I am."

"I'm sorry, I didn't mean to make you feel as if you shouldn't be in the class."

"It's not your fault, I guess I just feel like an imposter here," I admit.

"Me too."

"How did you get your scholarship?" The question is out before I can think about whether it's a good idea to pry. "I'm sorry, you don't have to answer that."

"It's all right, I don't mind. I don't fully understand it. I believe it's something to do with prophecies, but I didn't question it too much. A representative from the academy came to my parents' farm and offered me a place here. None of us were in a position to turn it down."

"It was the same with my family. The position, I mean."

"I think anyone who isn't noble would have trouble saying no."

"True. My parents are putting a lot of pressure on me to find a noble husband," I say, unsure why I'm admitting this to him when I don't know him.

"Ah, that makes sense. I suppose if I was a girl, my parents would want the same thing."

"Can they not want it from you because you're male?"

"I think they realise how much less likely it is," he responds. "I think they're mostly hoping that I'll find a princeling to make indebted to me so that he gives me a job once I graduate."

"That sounds like a very complicated plan."

"But not an impossible one."

"Would befriending someone not be easier?"

"Perhaps. Especially as we're not supposed to use titles amongst one another. That has to help with forming connections, right?" Conan asks.

"Mmm." I suppose he has a point, especially considering that the first friends I've made here at the academy happen to be princesses. Or maybe there are just so many of them in attendance that it's impossible to *not* end up friends with at least one royal.

"How are you finding it so far?" he asks.

"The academy? It's busy, but nothing compared to working in one of Father's shops when there's been a new shipment come in. And it's nice to not have to do everything for my sister all the time."

"Is she here too?"

I shake my head. "She wasn't offered a place." Something I'm sure I'm going to end up paying for when I return home. Kirsten hates anything that she deems will give me an advantage over her. Especially something like this that brings me into the company of royalty.

"I'm surprised. I'd have thought the academy would want siblings."

"I think it depends on why we're being offered a place in the first place," I point out. "And Kirsten is nearly twenty, she'd be too old to stay here for long."

"Ah, I can see how that would be an issue. I don't know why they don't offer us places earlier if they already know they want to."

"Maybe they don't realise until just before they do?" I suggest. "I'm not sure how it works with the younger students."

"Me neither, they're in another building. Probably so they don't have to worry about the older students teaching them bad habits."

"Or the level of supervision they need is different," I point out. "It's not like most of the students have had an upbringing where they've been involved in their parents' work up until now."

"Hmm, true."

"How will your parents get on at the farm without you?" I ask, trying not to feel too guilty about the fact my parents don't have me to rely on for the shops anymore.

"I have cousins, they'll barely notice that I'm gone."

"Isn't that sad?"

"Not if I don't have to milk the cows every day. There's this one cow called Bessie, and I swear that she hates me. Every time I go to milk her, she tries to bite me."

"Maybe you're doing something wrong?" I suggest.

He lets out a hearty chuckle, a warm sound that I like the idea of hearing more of. "I doubt it. I've been milking cows since I was old enough to walk unaided. Ma taught me precisely the way to do it without making the cows distressed."

"I'd never have thought there was that much to it," I admit.

"Then it is clear you've never milked a cow."

Guilt clouds my mind as I think on how presumptuous I'm being. "No, I haven't. I'm sorry, I shouldn't have passed judgement."

"It isn't a problem," he assures me. "I'm sure I'm going to make the same kind of judgements over the course of our friendship."

"So we're friends now?" I check, a little surprised by his forwardness.

"If you wish to be."

"I can't promise you employment after we graduate," I warn him, only realising as I do that I'm probably wrong, and there may be something I can offer then. But it's best not to bring it up again until I know him better.

"And I can't promise you marriage to a lord," he counters. "But that doesn't mean we can't enjoy one another's company while we're attending lessons together."

"True. I'd like that." I smile at him, hoping he can tell that I'm being truthful when I say it.

Before either of us can say anything else, our teacher walks into the room and knocks her cane against the ground twice. Everyone falls silent, though how we know that's what we should do is lost on me.

But it's clear that my education at Grimm Academy is about to begin, and I know I need to pay attention if I don't wish to risk insulting the wrong person.

CHAPTER 3

The ball is in full swing, with music filling almost every corner of the castle, and most of the students who are around my age are crammed into the ballroom chattering away and taking turns on the dance floor.

I wish I could join them, especially when I see Cordelia and Elisa twirling past with their current partners. They seem so graceful on the floor, especially when I am aware that I wouldn't be. I don't have years of dance training and an in-built elegance like they do.

"Would you like this dance, Astrid?" someone asks from behind me.

I turn, only half surprised to find Conan waiting with his hands behind his back and a slightly nervous expression on his face, like he isn't entirely sure whether or not I'll say yes.

"I don't know the steps," I say instead of giving him a straight answer.

"I don't either."

I let out a surprised laugh. "I was half expecting you to say that you'd guide me through them."

"Oh, I'm definitely not capable of that. We've had four dance classes. I'll be lucky if I can get the hold right."

I frown. "So why ask me?"

"Because I saw the way you were looking at the dancers and figured you'd turn anyone else who asked down because you weren't confident enough to dance."

"That's really sweet."

"So, will you do me the honour of a dance?" He holds out his hand.

Despite knowing my parents wouldn't approve of my choice of dance partner, I reach out and place my hand in his. The warmth of his palm is enough to soothe any worries I have about whether I want to be dancing with him or not, I can tell that it's going to be the right choice, even from one touch.

"We'd better not be going onto the dance floor, though," I warn him.

"I had somewhere a little less obvious in mind," he promises, drawing me a little way from the dancers and towards a private alcove. We can still see the rest of the students, but they won't be able to easily see us, making it perfect for hiding the fact we're not as confident in the dance we're doing.

Conan holds out his hands in a position resembling hold, and I step into it.

"I don't think this is quite right," I say, taking his hand and putting it into position on my waist. The firm pressure isn't completely unwelcome, and I find myself relaxing a little more than before.

"Now we start counting, right?" he asks.

"Will it help?"

He nods and starts to count under his breath, which I have to admit helps more than I expect it to.

We start to go through the basic dance they've taught us so far, neither of us saying much more than the odd instruction about the steps. I'm sure many of the assembled nobles would be horrified with how we're doing, but I'm pleased. We may not be doing it perfectly, but I can tell that I'm more at ease with the steps now I have someone who has to focus on them as much as I do.

"Are you ready to spin?" Conan asks.

I nod.

He lifts his arm and allows me to turn under his arm. My skirt flares out around me, making me feel as if I'm a princess, even amongst all of the royalty present.

I place my foot down to try and steady myself but almost fall instead. Conan reacts quickly, reaching out to steady me.

"Sorry," I murmur.

"It's all right, I shouldn't have suggested such an advanced move."

"It isn't your fault I don't have any balance."

"We can practise," he promises. "Maybe not now, but I'm sure the instructors wouldn't mind us using the dance classroom for it."

He offers me his arm, and I take it, allowing him to lead me away from the alcove to where the refreshments are.

I smile warmly at him. "That would be good. I want to catch up with my friends."

"Aren't they princesses?"

"Yes, but Cordelia used to live under the sea, I don't think she's very proficient in the dances they do here." Though she also doesn't seem to be particularly bad.

Conan raises an eyebrow. "A mermaid? I didn't think they were real."

"You believe in prophecies, but you don't believe in mermaids?"

"I wouldn't say I didn't believe in them, more that I was sceptical about their existence. I'm the same about dragons."

"I've never seen a dragon, so I can't comment on that."

He chuckles. "Is that how we're measuring things?"

"I'm not sure how else to," I point out. "Though I've never seen a fairy and I believe in them."

"You'd be a fool not to, I don't think they take kindly to people denying their existence."

"Would you?" I ask.

"Fair point. I wouldn't like people telling me I didn't exist either. I suppose it would be a good approach to assume that everything is possible until categorically proved otherwise."

"But how could you do that?" I ask. "You may not have seen a dragon, but that doesn't mean that they don't exist. You'd only ever be able to prove that something *did* exist, not that something didn't."

"That is the life lesson I will take away from our conversation this evening," he promises.

I find myself letting out an easy laugh, as I seem to have been doing with ever more frequency while I am in his company.

"Ah, it appears that my allotted time to spend with you is over," he says, nodding in the direction of my friends heading towards us.

"You can stay if you want to, they won't mind," I assure him.

"Perhaps you can seek me out again if you wish to attempt another dance," he says.

"I'll hold you to that," I respond with a bright smile.

He lifts my hand to his lips and kisses the back of it, sending a small flutter right through me in response.

"Until next time, Astrid."

I watch him leave, a little disappointed to be parting ways, even though the song ending has technically signalled that it is time for that.

"Was that Conan we spied dancing with you?" Elisa asks, curiosity written all over her face.

I nod. "He asked if I wanted to because he knew I wouldn't say yes to anyone else."

Cordelia lets out a small excited squeak. "That's so sweet of him."

I glance over in the direction he's disappeared in, but he's nowhere to be seen. "I know."

"I thought your parents wanted you to court a noble?" Cordelia asks.

"I'm not courting anyone."

"But you want to," Elisa teases. "And you want it to be Conan."

I let out a loud sigh. "It doesn't matter what I want," I point out. "My parents made it clear that they have expectations."

"But surely they don't want you to be miserable just to fulfil them?" Elisa asks, horror filling every word.

Cordelia stays unsurprisingly quiet. She's probably far more aware of what it actually means to go against her parents considering she's banished from the sea for supporting her older sister.

"It doesn't matter anyway," I assure them. "I'm not courting anyone, so there's nothing to disappoint them with, and nothing for me to be sad about."

Elisa seems as if she's about to argue, but Cordelia comes to my rescue by pressing a goblet of strawberry wine into her hand.

"We should make the most of the kitchen providing us with the good stuff," she says.

I flash her a grateful smile and pick up a goblet of my own, determined to enjoy the rest of the evening with my friends.

CHAPTER 4

I take a deep breath and pause outside the dining room, knowing that when I go inside, I have to face my family. I'm not sure why I'm so nervous about seeing them, perhaps because I'm aware that I'm not managing very well when it comes to their insistence that I come away from Grimm Academy with a noble suitor. Something I'm further away than ever from achieving.

"Astrid!"

I turn to find Conan hurrying towards me, causing my heart to skip a beat and some of my worry to vanish, despite the fact that he's technically part of the cause of it.

"Hey." I smile, hoping he doesn't sense my discomfort.

"I didn't see you in class."

"My family is visiting." I gesture to the double doors.

"Ah, that explains it. I brought you this." He holds out a single flower.

For a moment, the world goes quiet as I stare at the red petals in front of me. Is this how my prophecy starts? I've always known that it would start when I'm presented with a rose.

Except that this is clearly a poppy.

I let out a relieved sigh and reach out to take it from him, letting my fingers graze against his as I do. "Thank you, it's beautiful." I tuck the flower into my lapel, enjoying the way it looks there.

He beams at me, clearly pleased by my response. "I'll leave you to your family visit," he says. "I hope you enjoy it."

"Thanks. I'll see you later?" The hopeful tone in my voice isn't missed by either of us.

"I hope so." He smiles, "I was also wondering if you wanted to have dinner with me?"

"Like a date?" I ask, a surprising amount of excitement growing within me at the question.

"If you'd like that." He seems nervous. Maybe he isn't sure about how I'll respond.

"I would."

"Great." He beams widely. "I look forward to it."

"Me too."

He waves and leaves me alone, heading back in the direction of the classrooms.

I touch the poppy, trying not to feel too excited by the fact he's gifted me a flower. It's a small gift, but that doesn't mean it has less sentimentality behind it.

I push thoughts of Conan from my mind and enter the dining hall, knowing I need to focus on my family, at least for the next hour or so.

There are several groups of people in the dining hall, several with students already talking to them. I scan the room until I find Mother and Kirsten sitting at one of the tables.

My heart sinks. Why is my sister here? I hope she isn't trying to worm her way into the academy. Even if she's too old for most of the classes, I'm not naive enough to think that she wouldn't find some way of making my life a misery.

I make my way over, trying to keep the smile on my face, but already feeling the high of speaking with Conan fading away.

"Astrid, you look well," Mother says.

"Thank you," I respond, taking a seat.

"And by that, she means you've put on weight," Kirsten says.

I look down at myself, but don't see what she's talking about.

"Don't be unkind, Kirsten," Mother chides.

"I'm not being, I even brought Astrid a present." She holds out a flower, the second one I've received in the past ten minutes.

"Thank you," I murmur, reaching out and taking it, only to prick my fingers on the thorns.

My heart sinks as I realise it's a rose, and panic builds up inside me about the idea of my prophecy starting.

I glance at Mother, expecting her to be worried about the same thing, especially as she knows the details of my prophecy while Kirsten does not.

But instead of concern, she barely responds at all, suggesting that I'm simply overreacting and that this is nothing to worry myself about.

"She already has a flower," Kirsten says, pointing to my collar. "Where did you get it from?"

I reach up to touch it. "A friend gave it to me." I don't like the way the words sound, as if there's a half truth in them somewhere. Perhaps because it's impossible for me to think of Conan as *simply a friend*, even if we're not officially courting.

"It doesn't seem like a friendly gift," Mother says, eyeing it more closely. "Are you courting someone?"

"No." This felt like a safer statement, though if things continue the way I'd like them to, I suppose it won't be true the next time I see them.

The thought of officially courting Conan sends a small thrill through me, even if I know it isn't what my family want from me. Elisa's suggestion about doing what makes me happy may have been a little misguided in how it lined up with my family's desires, but there is something to be said about the choice for me personally.

"You should be courting someone by now," Mother says. "You've been at the academy for several months already."

"That isn't very long," I point out. "And they only hold balls every couple of weeks."

"What about eligible nobles in your dance classes? Surely you'll have a chance to talk to them then?"

"I'm not good enough to be in the dance classes with any of the nobles yet," I say through gritted teeth. I'm not sure why she expects me to be when I came here without any formal dance training. It doesn't bother me particularly, other than wishing I could be in the class my friends are in, but she still can't expect miracles.

Mother lets out a loud sigh. "I will speak with the headmistress. It seems that *another* donation is in order."

"A donation for what?" I ask, feeling slightly alarmed by the direction of the conversation.

"To get you moved to a better dance class," she says. "We're spending a lot of money to send you here, Astrid, you need to make sure it's worth it."

"Oh." Tears threaten at the corners of my eyes, but I manage to blink them back before they fall. I understand that my parents want me to make a good match, and that I stand a better chance of making one at Grimm Academy than anywhere else I could spend time, but they seem to want it at any cost.

Not for the first time, I find myself grateful they don't live closer, or I suspect they'd be visiting a lot more.

"I'll try to do better," I murmur.

"Hmm, you should," Mother says. "I expect that when you come home for Yuletide, you'll be courting someone that we deem acceptable."

"Do I get a list of requirements?" I murmur.

Her eyes narrow and her lips purse with displeasure. "I trust for you to know what is acceptable and what isn't."

I don't point out that it's difficult to know if she doesn't fill me in. Then again, I suppose I can make an educated guess about what level of noble they want me to be courting. They won't be happy with a second son, or someone who is the heir to a small manor. They're expecting someone with a title and vast wealth that they can exploit in order to make more themselves.

A deep sadness settles within me over the realisation that my parents don't seem to care about my time here at Grimm Academy for anything beyond what it can bring them. It doesn't seem to matter to them that this is about keeping me safe from my prophecy, or that I'll be learning things that could be useful to both their business and my future career. They don't even care if I befriend royalty.

All they want is for me to come home with a bounty of wealth. Knowing them, they'll probably wish to drain it dry.

I stare at the rose lying in front of me on the table, a deep sense of foreboding settling over me. My sister may not like me very much, and she certainly resents me for the opportunity I've been given that she never had, but she wouldn't curse me. Even if I believe she is justified in being angry that my parents never gave her the opportunities I'm having.

But as much as that may be true, the rose can still signify that my prophecy is about to begin. No one ever said that the person who cursed me is the same person who gives me the rose.

I just have to hope that this doesn't mean that my prophecy is actually starting. And if it does, that I'm going to be able to find my way out of it before it's too late and I end up trapped in an endless forest, unable to ever escape from the beast that hunts me.

CHAPTER 5

Excited shouts fill the castle as the three of us descend towards the dining hall to have lunch. Have we missed the announcement of a ball or event? I don't remember anyone talking about one in class yesterday, but that doesn't mean anything. Besides, I doubt a ball would gain this level of excitement. They're regular fixtures to life in the Grimm Academy castle, and the excitement surrounding us doesn't match that.

Elisa turns to me with a questioning expression on her face.

I shrug. "Don't look at me, I have no idea what's going on."

Disappointment crosses her face, as if she expected me to have the answer. I suppose I do try and make sure I know most of what's going on in the castle so I'm not taken off guard by things.

"Mati said something about a competition," Cordelia puts in.

"For what?" I ask, intrigued by the possibility that there's going to be some kind of challenge going on. Especially one I haven't heard of.

"Something about Bellpoint Castle. I wasn't really listening," Cordelia admits.

"Bellpoint? Are you sure that's right?" Elisa asks.

"I think that's what she said. Why, what is it?" She cocks her head to the side, looking genuinely intrigued.

"And why is it stopping us getting to lunch?" I mutter. We only have a short amount of time allotted to get it before our next lesson starts, and I can get grumpy if I take too long to get food.

"You haven't heard of the Bellpoint competition?" Elisa looks between the two of us as if she's genuinely surprised that we're clueless.

"Should we have?" If she thinks about it, she'll realise that neither of us have any reason to. While Cordelia has been at the academy for longer than we have, she didn't live on land before that, and the only time I've spent around nobility is the past few months.

"Bellpoint Castle and the surrounding kingdom don't use succession law to pick their heir. The reigning King or Queen calls for a competition when they're ready to appoint an heir. People between the ages of seventeen and twenty throughout the kingdoms can compete, and if they win, they're crowned the heir," she explains.

"And they become a princess?" My question comes out as a whisper. There are so many things in my life that would change if I could become royalty. For one, I wouldn't be the only one of my friends without a title.

And for two, my parents would stop pressuring me to start courting a noble instead of following my heart.

"Who can compete?" Cordelia asks.

"Anyone."

"So we could sign up?" Excitement builds inside me at the idea of being able to do this. It feels like I can take charge of my life in a way I never have before, all by taking part in a single competition.

"Yes, if we wanted."

"We should do it," Cordelia announces.

Elisa frowns and looks at her.

"It would be nice not to rely on Mati and her fiancé for the rest of my life," she explains. "And it's not like either of you have a kingdom to run either. We should all do it."

"I don't need..." Elisa starts.

"You're doing it," I cut her off, reaching out and drawing her towards the sign up.

"It would be better if one of you won," she protests. And while it's true that she doesn't need this in the same way as either Cordelia or I would,

I still don't like the idea of the two of us taking part without her.

"But if we're all part of the competition, then we can help each other," I say, silently congratulating myself on coming up with a reasonable argument. "And that way, even if you don't win, you can help one of us do it instead."

"Fine. I'll do it," she agrees. "But only so I can help you both."

We hurry through the crowd and join the back of the queue to sign up. I go first, signing my name with a shaky hand. I know it's unlikely that I'll win, especially when there are so many people at the academy who are better qualified than I am to become the heir of a kingdom, but it feels good to try.

The list already has several dozen names on it, as well as a note that there will also be competitors at the other academies too. Which makes it even less likely that I stand a chance at winning. Even Cordelia and Elisa might struggle and they have a lot more experience with being in this world than I do.

I pass the pencil to Cordelia so she can sign up too.

"Elisa? Are you all right?" Cordelia asks, holding out the pencil to our friend.

"Hmm? Sorry. I was distracted."

"I guessed that when you didn't take the pencil. But you should hurry up and sign up before anyone starts getting annoyed at you."

For a moment, I think Elisa might change her mind. Instead, she takes the pencil from Cordelia and signs her name under ours. "Done." She hands the pencil to the next person in line.

"Good. Now, let's go to lunch," I say. "I'm hungry." I slip my arm through my friends' and the three of us start to make our way through to the dining room.

Elisa bumps into someone and offers them a quick apology. I don't recognise the person she's walked into, but he's handsome, and she seems a little flustered, but in a good way.

I exchange a quick glance with Cordelia, who nods in encouragement and I slip my arm out of Elisa's so we can give her some privacy.

Well, reasonable privacy.

"Are we really going to go eat without her?" Cordelia asks.

"Definitely not," I respond. "We're going to wait here and make sure she's all right. We can't just leave her with a stranger."

"Even a handsome one?"

"Especially a handsome one. Don't they warn you about that in the sea?"

She shrugs. "There's never really any need. I knew the names of all the people in our kingdom."

"Impressive."

"Only if Bellpoint Castle thinks so," she counters. "But I doubt they care much about the names of merfolk."

"Perhaps not, but your memorising skills might come in handy."

"Oh, true. What do you think they're going to test us on?"

"No idea. But unless they decide to have a round about accounting and fabric sales, I'm not sure I'll be much use."

"You don't know that."

"I'm a merchant's daughter," I remind her. "I doubt I'm what they're looking for."

"You say that, but there's got to be a reason they look for their heir this way. Maybe they realise they're looking for someone like you, not a high-born prince or princess to take their place."

"Maybe." But I'm not sure I believe it.

Not that it will stop me from trying to win, I'm just not going to get my hopes up.

Elisa heads back towards us, meaning we can finally go and get some lunch. Hopefully, our teachers will understand the hold up and will go easy on us if we're late to class because our food was delayed.

CHAPTER 6

I wait by the double doors that lead into the academy grounds, trying to retain control over the excitement growing within me. Despite the worries about my prophecy, and my family's visit, I've also got a first date with Conan to look forward to.

As if summoned by my thoughts, he appears around the corner with a picnic basket over his arm and a smile on his face.

An answering one stretches over my lips and I raise my hand to wave at him. I know my parents wouldn't approve of us spending time together like this, but I can't bring myself to care. Besides, there's the competition to become the heir to Bellpoint Castle starting in a few days and I'm going to do everything I possibly can to try and win. That will mean that I can follow my heart and not have to worry about what my parents expect of me.

Or at least, it will in theory. I suppose the only way for me to know for sure is to win and find out.

"Hey," Conan says as he reaches me, pulling me from my thoughts.

"Hi. I see we're going for a picnic."

He nods. "I know it's nothing exciting, but the village isn't really an option." He doesn't elaborate, but I know the reason. The kitchens will give us the food we need for a picnic if we ask for it, whereas food in the village has to be paid for. I already worry when I spend any of the small allowance my parents give me, I imagine the feeling is much worse for Conan.

"You might think it's unexciting, but the kitchens make great food. And it's the company I'm here for anyway," I remind him. Feeling braver than the last few times I've seen him, I lean in and press a kiss against his cheek.

I suppose we haven't properly talked about what's happening between us, which means that we're not officially courting, and yet there's no doubt in my mind that it's what we're doing.

"I'm glad you think so," he murmurs, offering me his free arm as he does.

"Do you have a spot in mind for our picnic?" I ask.

"I was thinking that we could go down to the lake, have you been before?"

I nod. "One of my best friends is a mermaid."

"Ah, right. Plenty of reason to go there. Have you seen her tail?" he asks. "Sorry, that's an inappropriate question."

"I'm not sure it is. I think that's like asking if you've seen her hair."

"I'm not sure how it works," he answers honestly.

"Officially, me neither. I'm just going by what Cordelia and her sister have told me." Not that I've had many conversations with Matilda. She mostly keeps to her own group of friends.

We make our way outside, and I enjoy the warm sunshine on my skin. The path crunches beneath my boots, only adding to the dreamy atmosphere that I always feel when I walk around the academy grounds. Despite having been here for several months, I sometimes find it hard to believe that all of this is real and that I'm part of it. At times like this, it's easy to forget that my prophecy is a real thing that I have to worry about. Especially now that I've been given a rose. I haven't seen any other signs that my prophecy is about to begin, so perhaps Kirsten's rose is just that. A flower given in order to provoke a response from me.

"Are you taking part in the Bellpoint Castle competition?" I ask Conan, partly out of curiosity, and partly to take my mind off the morose thoughts that are beginning to make the rounds in my head. I need to focus on more pleasant things, especially if I'm going to make the most of our date.

"I'm not." He lets out a soft sigh. "It sounds like an amazing opportunity, but I don't think I have the skills needed to even stand a chance at winning."

"That's how I feel," I admit.

"You're taking part?"

I nod. "It seemed like a good idea a few days ago when they posted the sign up sheet, but the more I think about it, the more I'm questioning whether it's a good idea at all. Every time we have an etiquette lesson, I learn more about the things that I don't know."

"Ah, but don't they say that it is a wise soul who can admit that they don't know all there is to know?"

I let out a small laugh. "Considering we're all at the academy to learn, I think that means I'm among many wise people, and a lot of competitors."

"True, but I've met some of the students, and I'm beyond certain that they'll go into the competition thinking that they've already won."

"They'll be out by the first round," I predict.

"Probably. And that won't be you."

"I hope not. I'll have my friends to help too. We're doing it together."

"That will help, I've seen how well the three of you work together."

We turn down the path that will start to take us through the forest and towards where the lake is.

"So, how are your plans to make some lordling indebted to you going?"

"About as well as your plans to court a noble are," he teases.

"Ah, so terribly and to the point where you wish the scheme had never been cooked up in the first place?"

He chuckles. "That bad?"

"Something you don't seem to dislike."

"Of course not, it means that I get to spend time with you."

"And court me?" The question is out before I can consider whether it is a good idea to make what is between us official. It will mean that there can be no more pretending that I'm going to go through with my family's plans for me.

He stops in his tracks and turns, a serious expression on his face. "Is that what you'd like?"

"I agreed to this date," I point out. "And every dance you've asked me to share."

"I know, but I'm also aware that agreeing to officially court me will make your family unhappy."

"It will," I agree. "But their plan for me isn't what I wanted for myself anyway. Marrying a faceless, nameless, noble isn't going to make me happy." I leave off the implication that I think Conan *can*. He'll be able to read between the lines, but it's still better not to put the kind of pressure on him that a statement like that would. Especially when the decision isn't one I made for him, it was one I made for me.

"Then I would like it very much if you agreed to officially court me, Astrid."

My heart skips a beat at the words, making me feel even giddier than I thought I would every time I imagined him asking me. "I'd like that," I say.

"Good. Then we can start with the picnic, and then perhaps you'll allow me to escort you to the next ball?"

I nod, excitement building up inside me. I can't believe this is actually happening.

And I'm going to enjoy every moment of it.

CHAPTER 7

I hurry down the steps that lead to the entrance hall of the academy, my invitation scrunched up in my hand. I can't believe I almost missed the orientation for the Bellpoint Castle competition. Between everything going on, I almost didn't notice it in my chambers.

"Astrid," Cordelia calls, looking almost as flustered as I do.

Perhaps responding to the invitation is actually the first test. Hopefully, this means we've passed it.

"What's going on?" I ask.

"No idea."

"And where's Elisa?"

"Also no idea. She disappeared after dinner and I haven't seen her since. Do you think we're going to have time to go and get her?" Cordelia looks around as if trying to work out how long we're going to have before orientation properly starts.

The sharp tap of a cane against the floor draws our attention to the man waiting at the front of the entrance hall with a serious expression on his face, leading me to believe that we definitely don't have time to go and find our friend, especially when neither of us have any idea where she might be.

"Good evening, everyone," the man says once silence has descended over the two dozen assembled students. "I am Master John of Bellpoint Castle."

A small murmur runs through the crowd as the meaning of the meeting becomes clear.

"There are less people here than signed up," I whisper to Cordelia.

"Maybe they're doing it in rounds? Or they've disqualified some people already?" She glances around uneasily as if searching for something to confirm or deny her theory.

"Is that why Elisa isn't here?"

"I don't think so," she responds. "They have no reason to disqualify her, right?"

"I mean, she's already a princess, maybe that disqualifies her?"

Cordelia shakes her head. "Unlikely. I'm here. And I'm in the same position in the line of succession as she is."

"So nowhere near becoming a queen?"

"Unless something happens to her three older brothers, she'll be a princess her entire life. Same with me. I'd have to be forgiven first, and then something would have to happen to my siblings. It's just not likely to happen."

I nod. "Which means it's unlikely she's been disqualified." So where is she?

The cane taps against the floor again, demanding silence and attention. "You've all been selected to take part in the Bellpoint Castle competition,"

Master John says. "Your first task is going to be tomorrow morning at ten, and you should make sure to be prompt. If you're not, then you'll be disqualified."

"Is there anything we need to prepare?" someone asks from the front.

"No," Master John replies. "The idea of the competition is that everyone has an equal footing, and to do that, there will be no prior knowledge given of the rounds, nor will there be any chance to prepare."

"Which would work if everyone had the same experiences," I mutter.

"I know," Cordelia responds. "It feels like we're at a disadvantage simply because we didn't grow up amongst the nobility here."

Right, Cordelia has just as little experience in some of the things Bellpoint Castle are going to be looking for as I do.

"I look forward to seeing you all tomorrow," Master John calls, effectively dismissing us all.

"We should go find Elisa and make sure she gets the information," I say. "We don't want her to miss the first round."

Cordelia nods. "Hopefully, she'll have her invitation letter and we won't have to face her being disqualified. We're going to need her to be taking part in at least the first round or I don't think we stand a chance."

She isn't wrong, I think both of us are aware that our chances of reaching the final are drastically lower without Elisa's help.

"Isn't that Conan over there?" Cordelia asks, nodding towards the dining room hall.

Sure enough, the handsome scholarship student is standing in the doorway. He lifts a hand to wave when he sees me looking, causing my heart to skip a beat.

"I'll go find Elisa," Cordelia says, disappearing before I can protest.

I shake my head in bemusement, but I'm secretly more than a little pleased. Any time I get to spend with Conan is good as far as I'm concerned.

I weave my way through the students lingering in the entrance hall to talk about the competition, but barely register who any of them are. There'll be plenty of time for that once we're competing against one another.

"Hey," I say as soon as I reach Conan.

"Hi." He looks as if he wants to reach out and put an arm around me, but decides against it.

I'm not sure whether I like it or not. I haven't told anyone that we're officially courting yet, despite the fact it's something I'm excited about. The timing hasn't seemed right, and saying it out loud will make it real.

"I've been thinking," Conan says.

"Oh?"

"Your parents still want you to court a noble, right?"

I nod. "Have you found a way to get a title?"

He chuckles. "No, all the pressure is on you for the Bellpoint Castle competition for that."

"It would solve a lot of my problems," I admit.

"And add a whole host more. You'd have to run a kingdom."

"Not right away. I'd have time to properly learn what to do." At least, I hope that's true. I never actually asked Elisa if they do that, or if the winner of the competition is just expected to start doing the ruling thing as soon as everything ends. "Anyway, what were you thinking?"

"I know we agreed to officially court, but do you think we should keep it to ourselves for now?"

I frown, unsure how to take what he's suggesting. "Do you not want to be seen with me?" A pang of hurt worms its way through me at his suggestion.

"It's a bit late for that, Astrid," he points out. "What I meant is that your parents are going to have spies at the academy, right?"

"I assume so."

"So would it be easier if they didn't know we were courting? They'll probably already know that we've been spending time together, but you can tell them it's for a project, or that we're studying or something like that."

I frown. "I'm not sure I like the idea of it being a secret. Is that what you want?"

"I can't say it's a great feeling, but whenever I think about how it will affect you, I realise it's a small price to pay. You never know how these things are going to affect the competition either."

I want to tell him that it doesn't matter and that I don't care, but we both know that would be foolish. This is an opportunity like no other, one that means I can choose my fate and not be restricted by the circumstances of birth. And if our courtship goes well, that would give him a good place too. Something that I don't think will have escaped his notice.

"But we're still courting, right? You don't want to end this?" My voice shakes as I ask the question, making me realise just how little I want it to change.

"I would still very much like it if we were," he responds.

"Then we can keep it quiet for now," I say. "But perhaps we should arrange for a quiet date in the library tomorrow evening so I can tell you all about the competition?"

He smiles warmly at me. "I'd like that very much."

"I'll meet you after dinner?"

He nods. "I look forward to it."

I do as well, even if I know this goes against everything my parents would want.

Though perhaps that's one of the reasons it feels so good.

CHAPTER 8

Elisa smothers a yawn, but manages to make her way into the grounds with us. I'm not sure precisely what happened last night, but Cordelia said something about Elisa meeting with her brothers in the forest.

I suppose it doesn't matter, she got the invitation, even if she missed it, but we've made sure that she's here and isn't missing out on the opportunity to compete for the Bellpoint Castle title.

Nerves flutter within me at the thought of what's to come. I'm dreading the test ahead and discovering that it's something I don't know how to do. But I have to try my best. If I fail after doing that, then it's all right, I'll have tried and won't be any worse off other than being a little disappointed.

The other students are milling around outside the large, creating a nervous energy that I don't like the feel of. There are less people around than there were at the orientation meeting yesterday, but I'm not sure why that might be. Perhaps some of the early arrivals were taken somewhere else in order to keep it simpler.

Or maybe some of the others haven't arrived yet. We've made sure to set off in plenty of time, even with having to collect Elisa from her room.

"I'm glad I'm doing this with the two of you," Cordelia says, slipping her arm through mine while she does the same on the other side with Elisa.

"Me too," Elisa responds.

The three of us make our way inside the tent along with the other students. Barely anyone is talking as the weight of the situation starts to settle upon us all.

"Good morning, everyone," Master John says once everyone is inside.

I do a quick head count and find myself relieved to realise there are the same number of people here as last night. Or at least, roughly the same number. Some of them must have been inside the tent already, or have arrived just after us.

I'm not sure why I think that's a good thing when it means there's more competition for us, but I guess it means that they're not eliminating people before they've had a chance to prove themselves.

"I'm Master John from Bellpoint Castle," he reminds us. Though I suppose for Elisa and anyone else who wasn't there last night, it's an introduction. "And I want to welcome you to the heir competition. As I'm sure you're aware, this competition is being run at academies across the kingdoms. Each task will assess a variety of skills, and they will be used to judge you. The heir will be the person who we deem to be the most suitable.

The criteria for that will not be revealed for the purpose of fairness."

Does that mean I stand more of a chance, or less of one? It's hard to be certain.

Or perhaps they don't have set criteria and are looking for something else in their heir.

"Your first task will be to organise a seating chart for a banquet to honour the coronation of a new monarch. Each of you is going to be given a sheet of parchment including the titles of the people who are being invited, and a map of the banquet hall. You'll have an hour to place everyone in the right seats. Once you've completed the charts, they'll be collected and you can enjoy the rest of your days. We'll contact you all when the next task is imminent," Master John says.

Dread settles within me as I realise the enormity of the task. While I understand the importance of being able to properly do this, I'm not sure whether I have the knowledge to pull it off convincingly.

I suppose I'm about to find out.

Several students enter the tent and hand out scrolls and a seating chart to each of us in turn.

I thank the maid who gives me mine, though it does nothing to allay my misgivings. I glance at Elisa, who appears to be relieved, and then to Cordelia who seems as concerned as I am.

At least I'm not alone in that.

The chart doesn't seem to be too complicated, and the seats are organised in an orderly fashion. Though that's only going to be the half of it.

"You may begin," Master John announces from the front of the tent.

With shaking fingers, I unfurl the scroll the servant gave me and scan the information written inside. There aren't any names on it, but there are small biographies and basic information about alliances and rivals. Some of it seems familiar, and I have to wonder if they're real people, just with their names removed.

I suppose it doesn't matter, I need to put them in the right places at the banquet, and that will include taking rank and relationships into account.

I take a deep breath and put the newly coronated monarch in the right place, along with their spouse. I search the list to discover whether they have any family members on it, so I can put them in a position of honour. Even if they aren't the highest ranking guests, it makes sense to me that they would have good positions on the chart.

The more I get into it, the more I realise I know. Both because of my lessons here at Grimm Academy, and because of the stories I heard from father after he travelled, and from some of the clients at the shops.

It's actually amazing to think of what I know already, especially when I was so worried about it.

I glance over at my friends, unsurprised to find Elisa helping Cordelia with who to put where. The fact she's not instructing me the same way only adds to my confidence that I'm doing this right. I know she'd say something if she thought I was putting someone in the wrong seat.

I pause for a moment, unsure whether to put the Duke of Norwholing next to the Marquis of Dunmak, or not.

"Elisa?" I ask.

My friend looks up from her chart and pays attention to mine. "Switch them." She points to the Duke and one of the princelings from the Western Isles. "They'll both be happier with the other companions."

"Thanks."

"You're welcome." She smiles and returns to her own chart. With the time limit ticking away, we can't afford to waste it.

I'm not sure whether we're really allowed to help one another, though we haven't explicitly been told that we can't. Personally, I suspect they're watching to see who is capable of asking for help when they need it, rather than whose ego is too big to admit that they aren't aware of something. That's a quality I would want in a leader, so it seems logical to me that the Bellpoint Castle representatives would be searching for the same.

Which means that this isn't about getting the seating chart exactly right, it's about the method in which we do it.

I mostly focus on my chart, though I occasionally ask Elisa for her advice on what she thinks about a certain arrangement. Much to my relief, she continues to answer, and doesn't seem to grow weary with either Cordelia or I asking her thoughts.

Elisa would be a worthy winner of the competition, I'm sure of it. Even if she already believes she doesn't have what it takes to win.

"That's the end of the task. Please hand your completed seating plans in now," Master John announces far too quickly for my liking.

I stop working and stare down at my seating chart, hoping that it's going to be enough in order to pass this round and move on to the next one. I think I've done a good job, but without seeing the answers, it's impossible to know.

A servant comes by and collects my seating plan along with those of my friends. I hope they're not going to make us wait too long in order to hear the results.

The three of us leave the tent, all a little lost in our own thoughts. We're going to need to do something to distract ourselves, or we're going to end up dwelling on the test for the rest of the day.

"Do you want to head into the village now?" I ask once we're outside. "I've heard that the dressmaker has some new fabrics and I want to check them out."

Elisa shakes her head. "I need to go to the library. I have an essay I completely forgot about due."

"I'll come with you," Cordelia says. "I want a new dress for the ball next week."

Elisa waves goodbye to us and heads back up to the castle. We turn in the direction of the gates, only for Conan to appear on the path towards us.

"You know, I need to finish an essay too," Cordelia says, clearly lying. She always does her academy work the minute she gets it. I think she's partly worried about being kicked out of the academy.

Even so, I don't call her out on it, and let her disappear back to the academy, leaving me to talk to Conan.

CHAPTER 9

I fall into step beside Conan, sensing that something is bothering him. Perhaps he's rethinking last night's suggestion that we keep our courtship quiet for now. I don't mind if it is, I think there are advantages to not being silent about it.

"Can we sit?" Conan asks when we come across an empty bench.

I nod, smoothing out my skirts so I can sit without wrinkling the fabric. It isn't just vanity that makes me do it, but the knowledge of how difficult they can be to get out, and not wanting to subject the academy laundresses to the extra work. It's still surreal to me that I have someone else who will do that kind of thing for me here. I suppose on the off chance I do end up winning the Bellpoint Castle competition, I may have to get used to that.

"How was the test?" Conan asks.

"It was fine. I'm not sure how it went, though I'm sure we'll find out soon enough," I respond. "But that isn't what you want to talk about, is it?"

He shakes his head and lets out a loud sigh. "This is harder than I thought it would be."

I reach out and place a hand over his. "What is it?" I'm not sure why, but I'm certain he isn't going to end our courtship. Though I don't know where the confidence is coming from, and there's a chance I'm going to be hurt by the next words out of his mouth.

"You know that I'm a scholarship student?" he checks.

"Yes."

"And that I have a prophecy?"

I nod. "I have one too, if that helps with what you need to tell me."

He perks up, seeming almost relieved. "You do?"

"I think that's why I was offered a place at Grimm. My parents can afford to pay for my tuition, but I don't think they'd have let a merchant's daughter in without a prophecy too."

"You don't know that."

"That's fair, I don't. And maybe I'm being harsh on the administration to think they'd turn someone away simply because of their birth. Especially when they don't seem to do that."

"It's hard to be sure," he agrees.

"So you wanted to tell me something about your prophecy?"

He nods reluctantly. "I don't really know how to explain it."

"Why don't you start at the beginning?"

"There isn't really one," he admits. "I've never been told the full thing, only that I will start turning into a beast when the moon rises each night. And that if I don't manage to break the prophecy within one month, I will turn into a beast for good and I won't ever be able to return to human form."

My heart sinks. Not just because it's a horrible thing for him to have to deal with, but because of my own prophecy about ending up trapped by a beast.

"Astrid? Are you all right? You've turned pale," he says.

I swallow my nerves, knowing that I have to be honest with him. "My prophecy involves being chased by a beast through an eternal forest," I admit.

"Oh."

"Is it too much to hope that it's a coincidence?"

"Probably," he agrees. "How do you get trapped in the forest?"

"I'm not sure. That part has always been very hazy to me. All I know about my prophecy is that it'll start when I'm given a rose..."

"Which is why you paused when I gave you the flower the other day."

I nod. "Yes. It took me a moment to realise that it wasn't anything to worry about. Then after that,

I have a limited amount of time to break the curse placed on me before I end up wandering a never-ending forest being hunted."

"That doesn't sound particularly pleasant."

"No, I can't say I've been looking forward to it," I mutter.

"Is there any chance that the time you have to stop your curse is a month?"

"There is, but I've never been given a timeframe before," I respond. "So a month is possible, but I have no way of knowing for sure."

"That must be frustrating."

"As is a prophecy regarding a rose. They're a common gift."

"Hmm, true."

"I'm glad you wanted to share your prophecy with me," I say, meaning every word. It takes a great deal of trust in order to talk about it. While I know that they have them, I don't even know what the prophecies of my best friends are. "But why have you chosen to tell me now?"

"Because it's started," he whispers. "I've been turning into a beast after sundown for about a week."

My heart sinks. "A week? That's not much time left to find a solution."

"I didn't realise it was happening at first," he admits.

"Wait, a week ago?"

He nods. "Yes, why?"

"That's the day my family came to visit." Horror fills me as I realise what that means.

"I'm not sure I follow," Conan responds. "What would that have to do with my prophecy or the curse?"

"My sister gave me a rose that day."

"Despite knowing what roses mean for you?"

"She has no idea about my prophecy, my parents chose to keep her in the dark," I respond. "I dismissed it because I didn't think there was any chance that my sister was the one who cursed me."

"Does your curse state that the person who cursed you is the same one who gave you the rose?"

"No." Which is the realisation that I'm coming to. "And you started to transform into a beast the same evening?"

"I believe so."

"Do you think the two prophecies are related?" I ask. "I don't know enough about them to know how possible that is, but..."

"Sometimes things are too much of a coincidence to be ignored," he finishes for me.

"Exactly. Too many things line up for us to be able to ignore any of them."

"Precisely."

I take a deep breath. "What does it mean if they are connected?"

"Hopefully that one solution will stop both of us from suffering a bad fate." He flashes me a weak smile.

"Then we're going to try and do everything possible to find a way to break the curse," I promise. "Within three weeks."

He lets out a dry chuckle. "Definitely within three weeks. I don't want to turn into a beast for good. And I don't want to chase you around an eternal forest."

A shiver runs down my spine as I realise what extreme torture that would be, especially knowing how much he would dislike it, and have the constant reminder of what we both lost. Somehow, the knowledge that failure dooms someone else alongside me makes it all the worse.

"We'll figure it out," I promise, though I'm not precisely sure how.

"I hate that you're going through this, but I'm glad that I'm not going through it alone," Conan says.

I lace my fingers through his and give his hand a squeeze. "Me too." And I mean it. With both of us trying to work this out, it actually feels as if we might be able to fix the curse before it's too late.

CHAPTER 10

E very lesson feels like a distraction from the important task of trying to discover a solution to the prophecy that is threatening to take both Conan and I, but I know I need to go to them if I want to keep my place at Grimm Academy. Besides, there are rumours that while the staff at the academy aren't allowed to directly interfere with a prophecy, they often make lesson plans based on what they know their students need. The idea leaves a lot of questions in my mind, mostly about how they're aware of what's needed in the first place, but I suppose it doesn't matter if it manages to help people.

Helping students deal with their prophecies is something the academy is known for throughout the kingdoms. I've heard enough whispers about it from patrons of my parents' shops.

I leave the classroom and turn in the direction of the library, determined to spend the time before dinner researching. I find it very unlikely that I'll find an answer written in one of the books there, but if I don't try, then I definitely won't find what we need in order to change the future.

A hand clasps around my wrist and I let out a soft scream before turning and realising it's just Conan trying to get my attention.

He grimaces. "Sorry, I said your name, but I don't think you heard me."

"That's all right, I was lost in thought. I'm going to the library if you want to come with me?"

He shakes his head. "I need to show you something in the forest."

"Ominous."

"And yet you trust me enough to go." He grins. "I know it's close to moonrise, but one of my teachers said something while I was in class today that I thought might help us."

"Then we have no time to waste," I point out.

He starts to head towards the entrance to the castle, and I follow along behind. For a moment, I consider whether or not it's foolish for me to not be wearing a cloak considering the slight chill in the air, but with sunset meaning that Conan will no longer be able to speak with me, I don't wish to waste any time.

We make our way across the grounds and towards the forest. I don't feel too worried about going in there at this time in the evening. Everyone knows that while the forest contains all kinds of magical things and beings, there is nothing that can cause any of the students harm. I'm not sure whether it is because the groundskeepers look after the forest so well, or because there's an enchantment of some kind on the area, I don't think I particularly need to know.

"Where exactly are we going?" I ask.

"To a clearing I came across," Conan says. "I think it will help."

"How?"

He frowns. "I'm not sure. I just entered it and I got the feeling that I needed to bring you there."

"Sounds like it could be a trap," I half-jest.

"If we were closer to the end of our month countdown, then I might feel the same." He glances up at the sky and grimaces.

He doesn't need to say anything for me to know that he's nervous about the onset of dusk.

I reach out and take his hand in mine, giving it a gentle squeeze. Of all the people I've met since coming to Grimm Academy, I'm glad he's the one I'm going through this with. I'm not sure whether it is his steadfast determination or his reassuring presence that makes me feel more at ease, but I get a sense that when I'm with Conan, there's a chance that everything will turn out well.

I just hope I'm not wrong.

"This is it," he says, pulling me through a canopy of trees and into a small clearing.

"It feels magical here," I say, stepping further in and letting go of his hand so I can bask in the warm glow the clearing is giving off. It doesn't have the same coolness the rest of the forest does, and I'm reasonably certain that I can't feel the wind. "But what now?"

"I'm not sure," he admits. "It was just a feeling."

"Maybe it's the fairies," I say, a small amount of awe creeping into my voice. "They're supposed to live in the woods here. They might even be what we need in order to help us."

"Perhaps."

"Do you have anything we can give them as a tribute?" I ask, digging into my pocket and pulling out a couple of bonbons. It isn't much, but it should be enough for the fairies.

"I have some bread."

"That will do perfectly."

He holds it out to me and I take it, placing it carefully at the bottom of a tree along with the bonbons.

"Do you think it'll work?" he asks.

"No idea, but it's worth trying, right?"

He nods, seeming relieved by the fact that we're doing *something*. I have to admit that I feel the same way. It's hard to research and find nothing.

"Astrid, you need to leave," Conan says, a flash of panic flitting over his face.

"Why? It hasn't been long, and they'll be serving dinner for hours yet."

"Because the moon is rising." He glances at the sky.

I follow his gaze, surprised to discover how dark it is.

"I don't need to leave," I say. "You won't hurt me."

Indecision wars over his face, along with fear. I'm not sure if it's because of what he's about to become, or because he's scared about my reaction. It is of no matter, I'm going to prove to him that he's got nothing to worry about. I'm not going to turn away from him just because of his curse.

"Will you look after my cloak?" he says.

"Of course."

He unclasps it and then whips it around my shoulders in one smooth movement. I hold it close to me, trying not to be too worried about what I'm going to see. I'm certain he won't hurt me, and that he'll still be able to understand the fairies should they decide to come, but I don't want to see him in pain.

As if my thoughts make it begin, he lets out a small cry, and his whole body contorts in front of me. I wince and close my eyes, unable to watch him hurting. I only dare to open them when the soft whimpers have stopped.

A large beast stands in front of me, reminiscent of both a wolf and a bear while being neither. I reach out to touch his face, able to see Conan's kindness in his eyes still.

"I'm sorry this is happening to you," I say softly. "I promise we'll fix it."

He lets out an odd sound, though I'm not sure what it means.

"Should we sit?" I ask, turning around to try and find a good spot, only to freeze when I notice our offering to the fairies is gone.

Does that mean...

"Hello, child," an ethereal voice says from behind me.

I turn towards it, surprised to find a small creature with translucent fluttering wings perched on a branch at about the same height as me.

I've never seen a fairy before, but I already know what it is.

"Thank you for agreeing to see us," I say.

"You gave us an offering, child. We decided to return the favour by speaking with you."

"We appreciate it." I reach out and curl my hand into the fur of Conan's shoulders. I assume he's able to understand, but regardless, I want him to know that I haven't forgotten he's here.

"You wish to know how to break the curse placed over you," the fairy says.

I nod. "Is it the same curse on us both?"

"Yes and no. Your curses are so tightly linked that there is no telling them apart."

"Is that a good thing?" Worry fills me that we might not be able to fix our problem at all.

"To break the curse, you must plant the petals of the flower used to curse you in this clearing," she says, ignoring my question.

"The flower used to curse me?" I echo.

She simply nods. "The curse will be broken once the flower blooms."

I frown. "From the petals?"

"Yes. Plant the petals and wait for the flower to bloom. You must believe that it is possible or it will not happen."

I nod. "Thank you." I'm unsure what they mean about the flower that cursed me, or how making a flower bloom is going to break the curse and return Conan to his human form properly, but fairy magic is renowned for working in strange ways, I would be a fool not to trust the instructions they've given me.

I glance at Conan, wishing he could talk to me and reassure me that this was going to be okay.

When I look back to where the fairy was sitting to talk with us, she's disappeared, leaving me with nothing more than the hope that she's not sending

us on a wild quest that will only lead to disappointment.

CHAPTER 11

I yawn, trying to stifle the tiredness growing within me as the result of trying to work out what the fairy's words mean. I know that the rose was the start of my prophecy, but that doesn't mean that it's the flower that cursed me. If I was on better terms with Kirsten, perhaps she'd be able to tell me where she got it from, and that might help me work out what's going on.

But she has no idea about my prophecy, which means that there's no chance of getting her to tell me. For what feels like the first time, I find myself annoyed at my parents for choosing to keep it from my sister. Things might have been better between us if she'd understood some of the decisions they made.

"Are you all right?" Cordelia asks as we leave the breakfast hall. "You seem distracted."

"Just tired," I respond. "And a little worried about Elisa. Have you seen her yet?"

She shakes her head. "I stopped by her room before I came down, but she didn't answer. I'm guessing she must be doing something related to whatever it was her brothers needed her for."

"Does that mean she got the invitation for the next round of the competition, or not?" I glance in the direction of the stairs that will lead to Elisa's room, torn between going there to check, and going straight out to the tent.

"She will have done. And even if she didn't, she'd be annoyed at us if we got disqualified for being late," Cordelia says, already heading towards the double doors that go out to the grounds.

Somewhat reluctantly, I nod and follow her. I know she's right, but I'm going to feel awful if Elisa isn't there.

Students are already entering the tent, making it clear that we're only just on time. I search them for any sight of Elisa's familiar dark hair, but don't spot her until we're inside the tent.

She looks up and waves from the table she's sat at, leaving the two of us to claim the seats on either side of her.

"You weren't at breakfast," Cordelia says.

Elisa shakes her head and makes a gesture that I assume means she was asleep.

"Late night with Alaric?" I tease, knowing that she's been spending a lot of time with the fellow student.

Her eyes widen and she shakes her head again.

"Yes, yes, we believe you." I cross my arms and raise an eyebrow.

She shakes her head again. Is there a reason she isn't speaking to us any longer? She's answering our questions, so it doesn't seem as if she's angry at us. She mimes the act of writing, presumably to ask if either of us have anything in our pockets that she can use to write with.

Cordelia frowns. "What's wrong with your voice?"

Elisa presses a palm to her throat and looks sad. Ah, she's not speaking because she can't. If she's sick, that will be why she was sleeping, rather than spending a lot of time with Alaric. A pang of guilt goes through me at the thought of my teasing her when she was actually suffering.

"Oh no, maybe you shouldn't be here. We can cover for you?" Cordelia suggests.

"She can't do that," I answer for her. "There's only one chance to compete in this competition. If she doesn't do this task, then she can't move onto the next one and there'll be no way of winning."

"Her health is more important," Cordelia says quietly, checking around to make sure that no one is listening in who shouldn't be.

Elisa reaches out and touches Cordelia's hand.

"Only if you're sure," the mermaid responds.

Elisa nods. Which doesn't surprise me. She can be very stubborn. No doubt it's a result of growing up with three older brothers.

"Fine, but if you end up feeling worse after it, don't come complaining to me," Cordelia says.

I resist the urge to laugh, knowing that it isn't appropriate given the situation.

Another yawn tries to escape me, but I force it down. The last thing I want is for the assessors from Bellpoint Castle to think that I don't take this seriously enough to appear fully rested.

"Good morning, all," Master John says, drawing our attention to the front of the tent. "Today's test is simple. You need to prepare appropriate refreshments for a visiting ambassador. You will present them on your tables to be judged. You may begin."

Surprise flits across Elisa's face, probably because the task feels like a simple one.

Which it might be, for someone who has had experience in this kind of thing. For me, it's overwhelming to even start thinking about how I'm going to do this one. Especially when there's no indication of where the ambassador is from, or what kind of visit it's for. Somehow, I suspect a visit to organise a betrothal, and a visit to discuss a war, might be two different things with different requirements needed for the tea service presented.

Servants remove sheets from the top of several tables at the front of the tent, revealing all kinds of utensils, food, and tea blends. In other words, everything we might need in order to put together the perfect tea. Students get to their feet and go to examine the various objects. Some of them pick things up straight away, while others look more carefully.

I feel like I'm going to be the latter, but still manage to make the wrong choices. Especially with how tired I'm feeling.

"Why does this seem too easy?" I mutter, feeling more than ever that this is some kind of trap I'm not prepared for.

"I don't think it's supposed to be difficult," Cordelia answers.

Elisa nods in agreement.

"It's supposed to help them judge the best candidate for the heir of Bellpoint Castle, not be unbeatable," Cordelia continues.

"I suppose that makes sense," I agree. "But how do we make sure to impress?"

Cordelia shrugs. "I'm going to make up a welcoming tea like I would at home, but adapt it with what I've learned since coming onto land. I remember how the two of you reacted to seaweed tea, I'm not going to make that mistake again."

I'm glad of that, it was truly an awful tea.

I let out a sigh. "That's what I was afraid of. I don't think my go-to tea plans will be right for the situation."

Elisa reaches out and places a reassuring hand on my arm, managing to convey her support even without the use of her voice. I do hope she recovers quickly, though. I don't wish for her to have to suffer like this for long.

"Thanks," I say to her.

Once enough of the students have returned to their tables with their spoils, the three of us head over. While the challenge is timed, I don't think any of us see the point in rushing things and ending up fighting with other students in order to get the items we want.

An ornate teapot grabs my attention and I reach for it, eager to look at it better.

Before I can touch it, Elisa catches hold of my wrist and shakes her head. Without her ability to speak, I can't ask her why it's a bad choice, but I trust her when she says that it is.

"What about this one?" I set my hand on a much less fancy teapot.

She frowns and considers the pot I'm gesturing to before picking up another one and pressing it into my hands.

Relief floods through me. I don't understand what makes a teapot a good choice or a bad one, but I do understand that Elisa wants me to succeed, which means that this one is one of the best on offer.

Affection towards my friend sets in. I wouldn't be doing half as well in the competition if it wasn't for her.

I take the pot back to my table and set it down before returning for the other things I need. My confidence builds as I find myself in more secure territory with the tea itself. While I don't know much about the correct equipment to use yet, I do know plenty about how to tell the right qualities of produce. I carefully select the one I think will be best and head back to my table to start brewing.

It's only once I've started that I realise I should have paid more attention to the time, but my tiredness and uncertainty distracted me. If I'm not careful, my tea is going to end up either over brewed or under brewed by the time the judging comes.

And if that's the case, then there's nothing even Elisa can do to help me.

CHAPTER 12

I push open the door to my chambers and step inside, resisting the urge to collapse on my bed and go straight to sleep. I'm too aware that time is ticking, and with Conan stuck in the curse where he's not human during the evenings, time is even more precious.

I just wish that I had more answers about what's going on and how I'm going to stop this. It's certainly starting to feel impossible, even if I don't want it to be.

An envelope catches my attention, and I bend down to pick it up. I unfold the letter and let out a small groan of frustration at being eliminated from the Bellpoint Castle competition. I suppose I'm not all that surprised though, I was tired and distracted during the second round, and I'm sure my tea was far too weak to serve to an ambassador.

I sigh and drop it onto my desk near the vase with the dying rose my sister gave me. I should throw it out. I'm not sure why I kept it in the first place, only that something made me do it.

I pick up the rose only to catch my thumb on one of the thorns. I let out a soft hiss and pull my hand away, but not before a small drop of blood falls onto the white paper of the letter.

My eyes widen. How many times have they told us during our time here that curses are often sealed in blood? For some reason, I've never considered that would include *my* curse.

Or that I pricked my finger on this rose the day that Conan started turning into a beast.

I have no idea where Kirsten got this rose from, or who would want to curse me and be callous enough to use my sister to do it, but the rose that signalled the start of my prophecy, and the flower the fairy fairy mentioned as responsible for my curse have to be one and the same thing. I can't believe I didn't work it out earlier. Nor that I didn't think to bury some of the petals anyway, just to be sure.

I glance out of the window, relieved to see it isn't dark yet. Classes have only just ended, which means there'll still be time for the two of us to return to the clearing and bury the petals. I'm not sure if we both need to do it, but I'm not going to take any chances.

I hurry to the door and gesture for a passing servant, glad that they happened to be passing.

"Mistress Astrid," the maid says with a dip of her head. "How can I be of service?"

"Can you get a message to my friend Conan?" I ask.

"Of course, Misstress. What would you wish for me to tell him?"

"Tell him to bring a trowel and to meet me in the clearing. He'll know what I mean."

"Of course. I'll see that it is done." She doesn't even react to the strangeness of the request. Probably because the serving staff are used to the strange goings-on associated with an academy full of students dealing with all manner of prophecies. This probably isn't the strangest request she's ever dealt with.

She hurries off, either to deliver the message, or to communicate with another member of staff who will. I'm not too sure how that part of the system works, only that it does.

I return to my room and grab my cloak, not wishing to make the same mistake of going outside without protection from the cold again.

I turn my attention to the rose, setting it gently on a handkerchief and wrapping it up, being careful not to waste a single petal. I'm not sure how many we need to bury, but I don't want to lose any, just in case.

Satisfied I have them all, I place the wrapped rose in a basket and hurry out of the room. With moonrise fast approaching, we can't let any time go to waste.

Nobody pays me any attention as I make my way through the academy and out into the grounds. They're probably all too focused on their own troubles, or are preparing for the next round of the Bellpoint castle competition. I don't know how many people were eliminated in the last round, but I doubt that I'm the only one to get the rejection letter.

I push thoughts of the competition to the side, realising that I have more important things to worry about, especially when there's a chance I won't even be free in a couple of weeks time.

The forest is alive with the sounds of various creatures that called it home. I briefly wondered if any of the noises belonged to the fairies who helped us, but I doubt it. Everyone knows that the fairies only make themselves known to those in need. In all likelihood, I won't ever see one again.

I approach the clearing and let out a sigh of relief to find Conan waiting for me in human form.

"I have the flower. I think." I lift the basket by way of explanation.

"You think?" he echoes.

"I have no way to be sure," I admit. "But this is the rose my sister gave me the day you first transformed into the beast."

Understanding dawns on him. "I didn't realise you kept it."

"I don't know why I did. I don't particularly like roses."

"For good reason."

"I do like poppies though."

"For equally good reason," he answers with a wide grin. "But we should probably plant the petals. I don't think there's long until moonrise."

I nod. "That's why I sent a message instead of trying to find you myself. The servants know everything about where people are."

"They do." He holds out the trowel to me. "Would you like to do the honours?"

I nod, taking it from him. "Do you think we need to bury them in a specific spot?"

"The fairy didn't say as much," he points out. "But this is roughly the middle of the clearing, so I think it would be the best place." He gestures to a stone he must have placed earlier.

"All right, the middle of the clearing it is." I go down onto my knees and dig the trowel into the soft earth. It moves surprisingly easily, and I soon have a small hole that should be deep enough to bury the petals.

"Do we put the whole rose in?" Conan asks.

I frown, considering the question. "I'm not sure. The fairy was specific when she said we had to bury the petals, so if I have to guess, I'd say it's just those that we should be burying."

He nods and pulls the wrapped flower out of my basket. He sets it on the ground between us and uncovers it.

Carefully, the two of us peel off each of the petals in turn, trying not to do any more damage than the age of the flower already has.

"You kept it for a long time," Conan says.

I nod. "Longer than I should have done. Which is strange for me to have done in the first place," I admit.

"Do you..." he trails off.

"Do I?"

He lets out a loud sigh. "Do you think your sister is the one who cursed you?"

"I doubt she did anything on purpose," I respond, not as insulted by his question as I feel I perhaps should be. Mostly because I believe there is merit in his theory, even if I wouldn't want to admit it at first. "But perhaps she asked a hedge witch to inconvenience me or something. She had no idea about my prophecy, so won't have known how dangerous a flower like this would be to me."

"Hmm."

"You're not so sure?"

"I think it's a big coincidence, especially with how you've said Kirsten treats you in the past."

"It's not nice to think about," I admit.

"I'm sorry, I shouldn't have said anything."

"No, you should have done," I counter. "The moment you said it, I realised I've been wondering the same thing about whether she could have done this knowingly. I'd like to think that she couldn't. Or that she'd choose not to, but there's a part of me that isn't so sure. She's almost always resented me, though I'm not sure when or why it started.

I suspect it's only gotten worse since I came to Grimm Academy and got all of the opportunities she thinks she should have had."

"I'm sorry."

"Don't be. If anyone is to blame, it's my parents. They should have made sure she didn't feel badly about it. And they should have protected me better from her frustrations."

"Even so, I'm sorry that you can't trust her."

I offer him a weak smile and drop the last of the petals into the hole. "It doesn't matter anyway. We need to break the curse quickly, regardless of who the one behind it is." I push the first handful of soil into the hole, and gesture for him to do the second.

We fill it in and quickly pat down the soil.

I sit back and stare at the small mound of dirt, half expecting to feel something working towards breaking the curse already.

Unsurprisingly, nothing happens.

"Now what?" Conan asks.

"I'm not sure. How long do you have before moonrise?"

He glances at the sky, which has darkened quickly while we worked. "Minutes, I think."

Disappointment fills me at the thought of not getting to spend more time with him.

He reaches out and takes my hand in his, giving it a gentle squeeze. "This will all be over soon and we won't have to worry about moonrise again," he promises.

I nod, not wanting to point out that there's a chance this won't work and we're dooming ourselves by even trying.

"We'll come by every day around moonrise to see if the flower has bloomed," he says. "And if it hasn't in a week, then we'll have to start trying to find another alternative way of breaking the curse."

I shake my head. "This is the way. Remember what the fairy said? We have to believe that this is going to work in order for it to." I press my hands against the top of the buried flower and close my eyes. "This will break our curse."

Conan places his on top of me and repeats my words. "I have to go," he whispers after a moment.

I nod. "I'll see you tomorrow?"

"And every day after that, I hope."

I resist the urge to point out that even if we fail at breaking our curse, we'll still see one another every day, just in a much less enjoyable way.

I watch him leave, already feeling more alone. But now we've planted the rose petals, there's a chance that we won't be trapped the way we both fear. And that's something I'm sure we can both be happy about.

CHAPTER 13

With dusk getting ever earlier with each day that passes, it becomes a race against the clock to get to the clearing and check on the flower before Conan is forced to turn into a beast. I try to maintain the faith that the flower will do what it's supposed to, but there's a small part of me that is getting more and more anxious by the day.

The end of class comes and I rush to my feet, hurrying through the academy and out of the front door before most people have even finished packing up their belongings.

Somewhere else in the castle, I'm certain that Conan is doing the same thing.

"Astrid," a familiar voice says as I hurry down the steps of the castle.

I stop in my tracks and stare at my sister. "Kirsten? What are you doing here?"

"I was passing on an errand for Father and I thought I'd come visit." Something in her statement rings false, but I'm not sure what it is and I don't feel like I have the time to probe her further on it.

"I just have to do something for class, but if you head into the dining hall, I'm sure they'll feed you. I'll be back soon."

"Can't I just come with you?"

I shake my head, not wanting that for multiple reasons. "I won't be long."

She purses her lips, but nods and starts to head up the steps.

I wait for a moment, wanting to make sure that she's actually going before I set off. I don't want anyone knowing about the clearing, especially not my sister. I'm still unsure about whether I believe she would be capable of cursing me, but there's enough doubt that I don't want her to come with me.

Once I'm certain she's gone inside, I hurry down the path towards the forest, hoping that this is the evening I'm going to find the flower has bloomed.

I enter the forest, only pausing when there's a loud rustle of leaves behind me. I turn, half expecting to find Conan stepping out to join me. To my disappointment, he doesn't, and I dismiss the sound as nothing more than a rabbit or a deer going about their daily business.

I take the turn to go deeper into the forest and towards the clearing, stepping inside and letting out a shocked gasp and the glittering rose sitting at the centre. It looks much like the one my sister gave me, except that this one looks magical. I can't quite put my finger on what's different about it, but I can tell that it is.

"What did you do?"

Kirsten's voice makes me jump and I spin around to find my sister glaring at me, her gaze flicking to the rose. Her eyes narrow and anger covers her features, removing any shred of doubt in my mind about who is responsible for the situation I've found myself in.

"You cursed me." My voice cracks as I say the words. I think I've always seen it as a possibility, but not truly wanted to accept it. Kirsten may not like me very much, but I thought that family loyalty went further than that.

"How did you find out?" she sneers.

"I've known that someone was going to curse me for years, I just never realised you'd be the one to do it."

"You knew?" There's a shrillness in her voice that truly betrays her anger.

"There was a prophecy."

"You're one of *those* people? What am I saying? Of course you are. You're special little Astrid. Our parents think you're special, that you're pretty enough to snare a noble. But does little Astrid do what she's supposed to? No. She's too good to listen to her family's needs. She goes to Grimm Academy and falls for a farm boy."

Anger fills me. "I didn't dismiss my family's needs."

"Really? Then who was the boy I saw you talking to when we came to visit?"

I swallow hard, not realising that she'd seen me talking to Conan.

"Try and pretend he's a friend all you want, but I saw the way you looked at him. You went and courted down."

I hold my head up high and glare at my sister. "I would rather spend a lifetime with someone as kind and thoughtful as Conan, than ten minutes with someone who didn't give a thought to those who were below them in life. I don't know what will happen in the future, but I do know that no matter what he faces, Conan will remain faithful and hard-working. You may not believe that those qualities are what makes someone a good match, but they're important to me."

She lets out a sharp laugh. "You think our parents will let you stay here once they learn that you're not courting nobles like you're supposed to?"

"They can do what they want, Kirsten. I don't control them any more than you do."

I'm not sure what it is that I say which enrages her, but she lets out a high-pitched scream and launches herself in my direction.

A dark blur jumps from the forest and stands between us. It takes a moment for me to realise that it's Conan, but when I do, I reach out and touch his back, grateful for his steady presence, but disappointed that he hasn't yet turned back to his human form.

Kirsten's scream changes and she stops in her tracks, staring at Conan with fear in her eyes. "What is that?" she demands.

"*That* is one of the kindest, bravest, and most honourable people I've ever met," I respond, hardening my voice to her despite the affection I feel for Conan inside. "And you are the one who made him like this with your curse."

"I didn't do it."

"You cursed me, you cursed him. He became the beast that will hunt me for eternity while I run through an endless forest."

Something akin to horror flits across her face.

"You had no idea what curse you bought, do you?" I ask, pain lancing through me as I realise she not only cursed me, but she used magic she didn't understand.

"I just wanted to hurt you." Her voice shakes.

"You were successful. Leave, Kirsten. I don't want to see you again." For a moment, I consider whether her leaving is the best option. But I've heard there can be some severe punishments for curse casting, and I'm not sure I want her to suffer any of them. She's still my sister, even if she did this to me.

I don't think she's going to listen to me. She looks between me and Conan for one last time, and then turns and flees, not looking back even once.

I let out a sigh of relief and loosen my grip on Conan's fur.

"Do you think we need to touch the flower?" I ask him.

He cocks his head to the side, studying me intently.

I shrug. "I've no idea. But it can't hurt to try, right? If Kirsten is the one who cursed me, then that means this *is* the flower the fairy talked about."

He nods and makes his way over, carefully lying down so his front paws are stretched out, but not quite touching the rose.

I sit by him, leaning against his powerful shoulders.

"Together?" I ask.

He lets out a low rumble and the two of us reach out to touch the stem of the rose, my hand over his much bigger paw.

Nothing happens.

He lets out a frustrated rumble, and pulls his paw away, catching it on one of the thorns as he does. He lets out a small yelp.

"Let me look at it," I say, gesturing for his paw.

He lifts it up and I find the thorn, slowly easing it out of the paw pad. A smear of blood against the pale skin of my hands catches my attention.

"Blood," I whisper. "The curse needs blood." Without thinking twice about it, I reach out and purposefully press my finger against one of the thorns. This is how the curse started, so I guess it makes sense that it's how it will end too.

There's a slight prick of pain as I push down, but it doesn't last, and is replaced by a deep sense of relief settling over me, one that isn't in any way proportional to simply pricking my fingers.

I glance over at Conan to see if he's felt it too, only to find myself frozen in place when I realise he's no longer in beast form.

A wide smile breaks over my face. "It worked."

"It seems to have." His relieved expression reveals just how he's feeling. "Did you really mean the things you said about me to your sister?"

A blush spreads over my cheeks. "Yes."

"I'm glad you think of me that way." He reaches out and touches my cheek.

My gaze flits down to his lips, lingering there and thinking about what it would be like to kiss him.

He must feel the same, as he leans in, hesitating for a moment as if to give me a chance to pull away if I wanted to.

I don't, and I let my eyes flutter closed as his lips press against mine.

The unspoken relief, along with the affection that's built up over our brief courtship, come through the kiss, leaving me with a warm feeling I can't ignore, and the knowledge that I definitely don't want what we share to end.

CHAPTER 14

I fiddle with the fabric of my dress, worrying about speaking with the headmistress this late in the evening. I hate to think that she's been disturbed simply because of my prophecy.

I ramble through my account of the past few weeks, trying to include everything except for the kiss I shared with Conan. That's just for us, and doesn't seem to be particularly relevant to the events of my prophecy.

"Have you told me everything, Astrid?" she asks.

"Mmhmm."

"Very well." She pulls a large tome towards her, reminding me of what Cordelia said about there being a book of prophecy in the headmistress' office. I wonder if this is it. "What do you wish to be done about your sister?" she asks.

"Done?" I echo.

The headmistress nods. "You are well within your rights to demand a severe punishment for what she's done."

"I don't want that," I blurt. "I know what she did was wrong, but she seemed to be genuinely shocked by the consequences of it, and I don't think she'll do it again." More than that, I doubt my parents would ever forgive me if anything happened to Kirsten. Besides, the way that I see it, this is at least partly their fault and not Kirsten's.

"Very well. I will amend the report to say that we are unaware of the person who cursed you," she says, making a note on the sheet in front of her.

"You can do that?"

A small smile pulls at the corners of her lips. "I can do a great many things, Astrid."

"Oh." I sit back in my seat, a little overwhelmed by everything that's happening, and what it means for me.

"Do you have any questions for me?" the headmistress asks.

"What happens now? You offered me a place here because of my prophecy, but it's over now. My parents are probably going to want to withdraw me too." Especially once they find out about Conan.

"Ah, there you're in luck. Because you helped another student avoid their prophecy, you are able to stay here on a complete scholarship. There is no longer any need for fees."

"So even if my parents decide they wish to stop paying..."

"You can continue to study here. As can Conan."

Hope blooms within me. "But I didn't really stop his prophecy, because it was the same as mine."

"Not according to the book." She turns it towards me and gestures to the page on the right.

My name is written along the top, and all of the details of what happened appear beneath it, along with the word *avoided*.

The page next to it has the same information, but for Conan instead of me.

"How does this work?" I ask, touching the page.

"The only answer I can give is magic."

"Because you can't say more, or you don't know more?"

The headmistress chuckles. "That is a mystery I will leave it to you to solve." She seems somewhat amused. "Now, if that's everything, you may take your leave. Please ask Conan to step inside when you do." She gestures to the door.

"Thank you." I hastily get to my feet, hoping she isn't about to change her mind about letting me stay.

I go through it and find a relieved Conan waiting in the chairs opposite.

"How did it go?" he asks.

"Well," I say. "I get to stay here."

His eyes widen and hope blooms within me. "And me?"

I nod.

He grins widely and hurries over to pull me into his arms, kissing the top of my head affectionately.

"She wants to speak to you now," I say. "But maybe afterwards, we can go and get something to eat? I'm starved."

"That sounds like a good plan," he agrees. "I won't be long." For a moment, I think he's going to kiss me again, but he must decide this isn't the right place for it and disappears into the headmistress' office.

I let out a loud sigh and drop into his vacated chair, still in a little bit of a daze about what's happened, and the fact that something I've been worrying about for most of my life is completely over.

The future is an unknown thing, and I'm sure my parents are going to have a few choice things to say about the way things have played out, particularly if Kirsten has decided not to go home, and I have to wonder if things can ever be fixed between us.

But even if things can't be the same at home, that doesn't matter. I have my friends, and I have a potential future with Conan. If either Cordelia or Elisa manage to win the Bellpoint Castle competition, then I'm sure they'll be able to give me a good living as a lady-in-waiting to them. Or even something more lowly than that. I'm not the best seamstress, but I know enough about the process, and fabrics, in order to run a team of skilled workers.

I lose track of the time as I sit and wait for Conan to emerge, especially as I allow myself to completely disappear into my thoughts of what might be.

It isn't until he steps out of the headmistress' office that I realise I should stop worrying about the future for a moment and enjoy the present, especially when it involves good company, good friends, and a courtship like I could never have before imagined.

I rise to my feet and allow him to slip his arm around my waist.

"I think the dining room might be done serving dinner, but we can ask the kitchens for some food," he suggests.

I nod. "There'll be a nice fire going in my room if we want some privacy while we eat."

He raises an eyebrow. "I don't think I'm allowed in there."

"Oh, most people ignore that rule. Apparently, no one has ever been punished for it. Probably because they realise privacy is important."

"Or they're worried about angry Kings and Queens."

I let out an amused laugh. "To be fair, that feels wise. I'd be scared of them too."

"Then we shall take advantage of it and have dinner just the two of us."

"I'd like that." I'm smiling like a fool as we make our way down to the kitchens, but I don't care. Everyone can know how happy I am, and how much of a difference it makes to finally be prophecy free.

CHAPTER 15

Two pieces of paper slide under my door, and I let out a small groan of frustration as I realise that there isn't any peace here at Grimm Academy. Somehow, nothing actually changed now that my prophecy is over. I still have to go to class, and I still need to do everything else too.

I open the first of my two letters. The hand-writing is instantly recognisable as belonging to my mother, which only makes me nervous about what I'm going to find inside. I scan the words, tears pricking at the corners of my eyes as they register.

I suppose I should have expected my family to be angry at me, but it seems as if Kirsten has spun them a web of lies intermixed with some truth and failed to admit that she was the one who cursed me in the first place, making my accusations of her completely justified, rather than unreasonable as Mother calls them.

Though her main complaint seems to be about me openly courting someone she deems to be my inferior.

I scrunch up the letter and throw it into the fire, not even watching as the flames turn it into ash and dust. I understand that she's frustrated with me for not making a noble match, but that shouldn't be a reason to cut me off from my family.

I take a deep breath. It's going to be all right. I've had more support from the friends I've made at the academy than I've had from my family anyway, especially when it comes to working out exactly who I want to be

I turn the second letter over in my hands, half expecting it to be from Father giving me the same disapproving lecture as Mother did. But, while the handwriting is familiar, it belongs to Elisa and not to any of my family members.

I tear it open eagerly, a little confused by why my friend would be writing to me instead of coming by my room.

A small squeal of excitement escapes me as I read the single line that says she's able to speak again and wants me to come to her room so she can explain everything. I'm on my feet in an instant, and racing out of my room to get to hers.

I almost run into Cordelia outside of Elisa's room, which isn't surprising. She must have gotten the same letter.

We don't even bother knocking and push through the door and into our friend's room.

"You can talk again?" I blurt, almost startling the maid already in the room setting down a tea set.

"I can, yes," Elisa says, a wide smile on her face that looks something akin to the way I've been feeling in the past few days.

"Then you need to tell us absolutely everything," I instruct. "Start at the beginning and don't leave anything out."

Cordelia hurries herself to pour tea, handing us each a cup in turn and waiting patiently for Elisa to recount everything that's been going on.

I stare with wide eyes as she recounts a tale almost as strange as mine about her prophecy, and the reason she wasn't able to speak during it. "I'm sorry that I didn't tell you straight away," she says once she's come to the end of it. "I wanted to, but I didn't want to put either of you in danger. And I didn't know *how* to say it. I know we haven't really talked about our prophecies much."

"We should change that," I say quietly. "Because I also have something to admit about prophecies."

"Oh?"

"I, erm, managed to stop mine a few days ago." I should have told them sooner, but Elisa has been really distracted with what turned out to be her prophecy.

The two of them exchange confused glances. "You stopped your prophecy?"

"It's why I ended up kicked out of the Bellpoint Castle competition. I wasn't paying enough attention, even after you helped me with the tea set up."

"Wait, you're out of the competition?" Elisa asks.

I frown, did I not tell her that? I thought I did. "Yes, earlier this week."

"I'm sorry."

I shrug. "Don't be. Conan finally asked me if I'd officially court him, so it was worth it."

"The same Conan you keep dancing around because you're worried your parents will expect you to come home engaged to a noble?"

"Yes, but I've decided that I don't care. And if they do, then I'll just convince one of you to give me a title once you're the heir to Bellpoint Castle." I feel bad for lying about my parents' acceptance, but I don't think I'm ready to talk about the fact they want to disown me just yet. Especially when there's a small part of me that's hoping they're going to change their minds, however futile that might seem.

"That will be up to Cordelia," Elisa says.

"You have as much of a chance of winning as I do," the mermaid counters.

"I really don't. I got my rejection letter just now." She nods towards her desk, which must be where her rejection letter is. "I imagine they weren't too impressed by me worrying about my prophecy either."

"This doesn't bode well for me," Cordelia mutters.

"Which is why we're going to change how we've been doing things," Elisa says. "We're going to make sure you win."

"And that you don't fall afoul of your prophecy either," I add. I know she has one, but we've not really talked about it any more than we've talked about either mine or Elisa's, and I think that needs to change.

"Exactly. And now the two of us aren't going to be taking attention away from you while you're completing the tasks, it's going to be even better. You'll shine so brightly, no one will ever be able to look past you."

Cordelia laughs nervously. "You don't know that. I have all the other contestants at the other academies to beat too."

"But none of them have your secret weapon," I point out. "Us."

"You really think I stand a chance of winning this?" Something about the way she asks makes it seem as if she's finally accepting the fact that she might actually win.

"I've thought as much from the beginning," Elisa says.

"Me too. And it'll be good for you and Matilda if you win too," I add. Her sister is just as banished from the sea as my friend is.

Cordelia sighs. "I know. Mati's been amazing, and Lewis has been trying his best to accommodate both of us, but I don't think he meant to gain a little sister when he proposed to Mati. It would be good to be the one providing for myself."

"Even more reason for us to make sure it happens," Elisa says.

I raise my teacup. "To Cordelia, the future Queen of Bellpoint Castle."

"To Queen Cordelia," Elisa echoes, raising her own.

Our friend blushes, but actually joins in as the three of us clink our teacups together.

The sadness over my parents' decision somewhat fades away as I realise I've never felt more at home than when I'm with the two of them. Cordelia is just as displaced as I am, and that means that even if she doesn't become the heir to Bellpoint Castle, we can simply go and serve Elisa wherever she ends up.

Coming to Grimm Academy hasn't just rid me of the prophecy that's haunted a good part of my life, it's found me a true family that I know will last a lifetime.

***

Thank you for reading *Princess Of Petals*, I hope you enjoyed it. You can continue the series with Elisa's story in *Princess Of Feathers*, a retelling of the Wild Swans.

AUTHOR NOTE

Thank you for reading *Princess Of Petals*, I hope you enjoyed it!

I never thought I'd write a Beauty and the Beast retelling, mostly because it was never a fairy tale I connected with growing up (despite the love of books I share with the Disney version of the heroine). But ever since starting the Grimm Academy series, a lot of readers have asked me for a retelling of this particular fairy tale, and once I started researching, I found the direction I wanted to go.

I discovered that there were many versions of the story, but they mostly had a few things in common. The youngest daughter of a man asks for something that grows, most often a rose, and that causes her to meet the beast. In some versions, meeting the beast seems to be voluntary on the daughter's part, in others, she is forced into it. In almost all of the stories, the main character has a sister who is jealous of her, which is what I chose to use as the basis for Astrid's story.

Both Elisa and Cordelia will also get their stories in *Princess Of Feathers* and *Princess Of Scales* respectively, and Cordelia's older sister, Matilda/Mati (who was mentioned a few times), also has her own story in *Song Of Seas*.

If you want to keep up to date with new releases and other news, you can join my Facebook Reader Group or mailing list.

Stay safe & happy reading!

- Laura

ALSO BY LAURA GREENWOOD

Signed Paperback & Merchandise:

You can find signed paperbacks, hardcovers, and merchandise based on my series (including stickers, magnets, face masks, and more!) via my website.

Series List:

* denotes a completed series

The Obscure World

A paranormal & urban fantasy world where supernaturals live out in the open alongside humans. Each series can be read on its own, but there are cameos from past characters and mentions of previous events.

<u>Cauldron Coffee Shop</u> - <u>Broomstick Bakery</u> - <u>Obscure Academy</u> - <u>The Shifter Season</u> - <u>Grimalkin Academy</u>* - <u>City Of Blood</u>* - <u>Grimalkin Vampires</u>* - <u>Supernatural Retrieval Agency</u>* - <u>The Black Fan</u>* - <u>Sabre Woods Academy</u>* - <u>Scythe Grove Academy</u>* – <u>Ashryn Barker</u>*

The Forgotten Gods World

A fantasy romance world based on Egyptian mythology.

<u>Forgotten God</u>

The Egyptian Empire

A modern fantasy world set in an alternative timeline where the Egyptian Empire never fell.

<u>The Apprentice Of Anubis</u>

The Paranormal Council Universe

A paranormal romance & urban fantasy world where paranormals are hidden away from the human world, and are in search of their fated mates. Each series can be read on its own, but there are cameos from past characters and mentions of previous events.

The Paranormal Council Series* - The Fae of the Paranormal Council Universe* - Paranormal Criminal Investigations* - The Necromancer Council*

Other Series

Purple Oasis (with Arizona Tape) - Grimm Academy - Beyond The Curse* - Untold Tales* - The Dragon Duels* - Speed Dating With The Denizens Of The Underworld (shared world) - Seven Wardens* (with Skye MacKinnon) - Tales Of Clan Robbins (co-written with L.A. Boruff) - Firehouse Witches* (with Lacey Carter Andersen & L.A. Boruff) - Mountain Shifters* (with Lainie Anderson)

Twin Souls Universe

A paranormal romance & urban fantasy world co-written with Arizona Tape. Each series can be read on its own, but there are cameos from past characters and mentions of previous events.

Amethyst's Wand Shop Mysteries - Twin Souls* - The Vampire Detective*

About Laura Greenwood

Laura is a USA Today Bestselling Author of paranormal, fantasy, urban fantasy, and contemporary romance. When she's not writing, she drinks a lot of tea, tries to resist French macarons, and works towards a diploma in Egyptology. She lives in the UK, where most of her books are set. Laura specialises in quick reads, whether you're looking for a swoonworthy romance for the bath, or an action-packed adventure for your latest journey, you'll find the perfect match amongst her books!

Follow Laura Greenwood

Website: www.authorlauragreenwood.co.uk

Mailing List: https://www.authorlauragreenwood.co.uk/p/book-sign-up.html

Facebook Group: http://facebook.com/groups/theparanormalcouncil

Facebook Page: http://facebook.com/authorlauragreenwood

Bookbub: www.bookbub.com/authors/laura-greenwood